Dear Parent:

Congratulations! Your child is taking the first steps on an exciting journey. The destination? Independent reading!

STEP INTO READING® will help your child get there. The program offers five steps to reading success. Each step includes fun stories and colorful art. There are also Step into Reading Sticker Books, Step into Reading Math Readers, Step into Reading Write-In Readers, Step into Reading Phonics Readers, and Step into Reading Phonics First Steps! Boxed Sets—a complete literacy program with something for every child.

Learning to Read, Step by Step!

Ready to Read Preschool–Kindergarten
- big type and easy words • rhyme and rhythm • picture clues

For children who know the alphabet and are eager to begin reading.

Reading with Help Preschool–Grade 1
- basic vocabulary • short sentences • simple stories

For children who recognize familiar words and sound out new words with help.

Reading on Your Own Grades 1–3
- engaging characters • easy-to-follow plots • popular topics

For children who are ready to read on their own.

Reading Paragraphs Grades 2–3
- challenging vocabulary • short paragraphs • exciting stories

For newly independent readers who read simple sentences with confidence.

Ready for Chapters Grades 2–4
- chapters • longer paragraphs • full-color art

For children who want to take the plunge into chapter books but still like colorful pictures.

STEP INTO READING® is designed to give every child a successful reading experience. The grade levels are only guides. Children can progress through the steps at their own speed, developing confidence in their reading, no matter what their grade.

Remember, a lifetime love of reading starts with a single step!

Special thanks to Rob Hudnut, Tiffany J. Shuttleworth, Vicki Jaeger, Monica Okazaki, Luke Carroll, Anita Lee, Julie Puckrin, Walter Martishius, Derek Goodfellow, Pam Prostarr, Aeron Kline, Conrad Chow, Lester Chung, Allan Pantoja, Kelsey Ayukawa, Eric Wong, Greg Montgomery, Ryan Singh, Sarah Miyashita, Winston Fan, Karl Bildstein, and Sean Newton

Published in the United States by Random House Children's Books, a division of Random House, Inc., New York, and in Canada by Random House of Canada Limited, Toronto.

Visit us on the Web!
www.stepintoreading.com
www.barbie.com

Educators and librarians, for a variety of teaching tools, visit us at
www.randomhouse.com/teachers

Library of Congress Cataloging-in-Publication Data
Webster, Christy.
Mariposa / adapted by Christy Webster ; based on the original screenplay by Elise Allen.
p. cm. — (Barbie) (Step into reading. Step 2)
ISBN 978-0-375-85198-8 (trade) — ISBN 978-0-375-95198-5 (lib. bdg.)
I. Allen, Elise. II. Title. PZ7.W38977Mar 2008 [E]—dc22 2007033873

Printed in the United States of America

10 9 8 7 6 5

First Edition

STEP INTO READING®

Adapted by Christy Webster

Based on the original screenplay
by Elise Allen

Random House New York

Bibble is going to visit
his friend Dizzle.
He is scared to meet
Dizzle's friends.

Elina tells him a story
to make him feel better.

Mariposa is
a butterfly fairy.
She lives in a land
called Flutterfield.
She likes to read.
She reads about the world
outside Flutterfield.

Mariposa works
for two sisters,
Rayna and Rayla.

One night,
the Prince flies
to see Mariposa.
He needs her help!
The Queen is sick.

A fairy named Henna
wants to rule Flutterfield.
Henna has poisoned
the Queen!

Mariposa has read
about the outside world.
The Prince asks her
to find the cure.

Rayna and Rayla
want to go, too.
The three fairies
fly away.

Soon they meet
a Meewah named Zinzie.
Zinzie helps them.

She leads them
to the mermaids.
The mermaids know
where to find the cure.

The friends swim
with the mermaids.
The mermaids tell them
the cure is in a cave.

At last, the fairies
find the cave.
It is full of Skeezites!

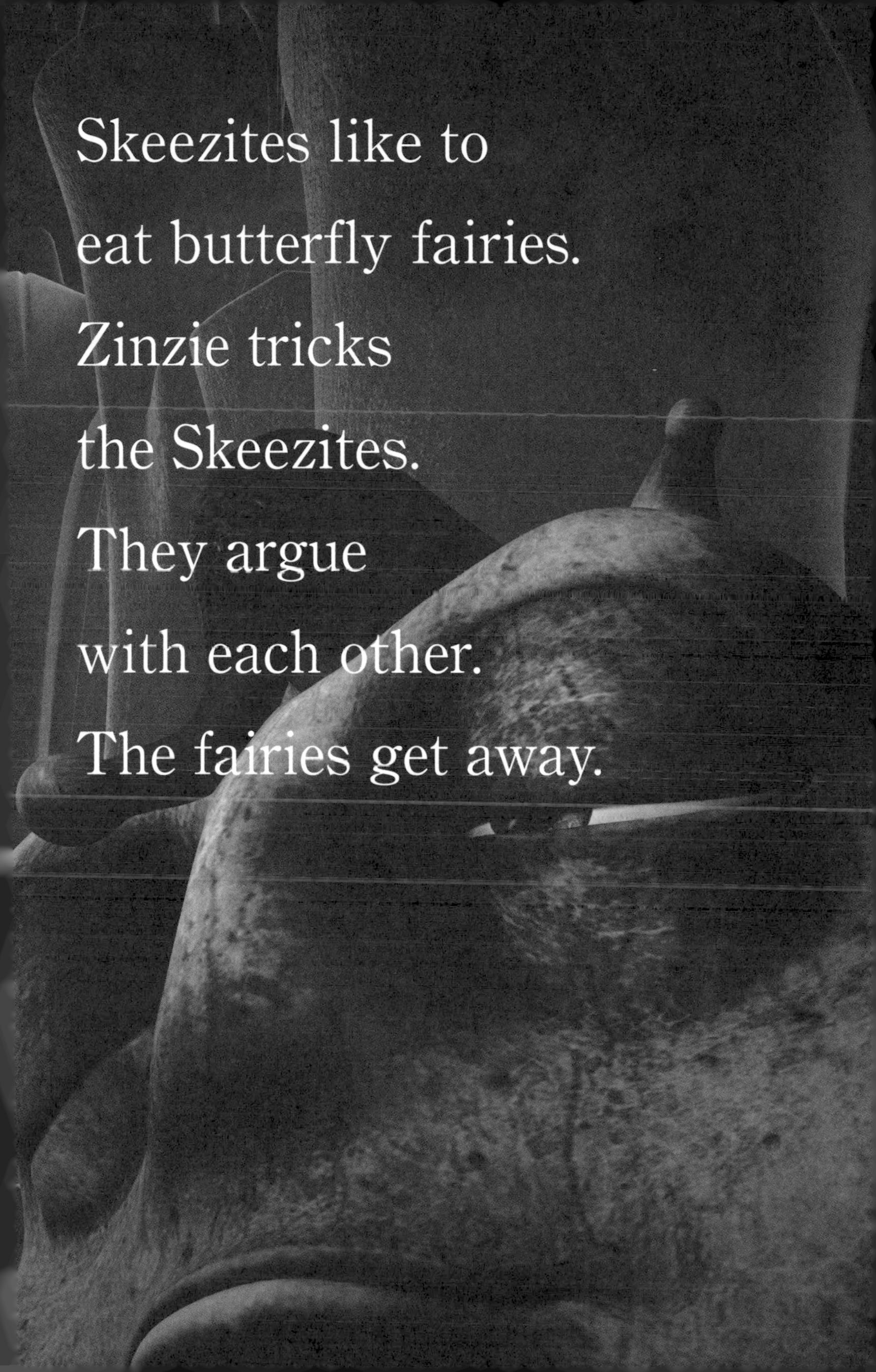

Skeezites like to
eat butterfly fairies.
Zinzie tricks
the Skeezites.
They argue
with each other.
The fairies get away.

The friends go deeper
inside the cave.
But only one fairy
is allowed to go on.
Mariposa is the one.

Mariposa must choose
the right star
to reveal the cure.
She does!
She is rewarded
with big new wings.

The friends bring
the cure to the palace.
Henna sees them.
She tries to stop them.

Henna is too late.
Mariposa gives the cure
to the Queen.

It works!

The Queen is better.

But Henna escapes.

The Queen thanks
Mariposa and her friends.

She gives them gifts
for their bravery.

Mariposa takes off
for more adventures
with her friends!

Bibble likes the story.
He is ready to make
new friends, too!